Orchard Books, an imprint of Scholastic Inc.
557 Broadway, New York, NY 10012

Printed in Singapore 46
Printed and bound by Phoenix Color Corp.
Book design by Barbara Powderly
The text of this book is set in 16 point Ellington.
The illustrations are watercolor.

10

Library of Congress Cataloging-in-Publication Data
Bloom, Becky. Wolf! / by Becky Bloom; illustrated by Pascal Biet. p.   cm.
Summary: A wolf learns to read in order to impress a group of farmyard animals he has met.
ISBN 0-531-30155-9 (trade : alk. paper).—ISBN 0-531-33155-5 (lib. : alk. paper)
[1. Literacy—Fiction. 2. Books and reading—Fiction. 3. Wolves—Fiction.
4. Domestic animals—Fiction.] I. Biet, Pascal, ill. II. Title.
PZ7.B47815Wo 1998 [E]—dc21 98-42421

WOLF!

by
Becky Bloom

illustrated by
Pascal Biet

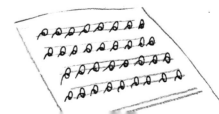

ORCHARD BOOKS
New York

After walking for many days, a wolf wandered into a quiet little town. He was tired and hungry, his feet ached, and he had only a little money that he kept for emergencies.

Then he remembered. There's a farm outside this village, he thought. I'll find some food there. . . .

As he peered over the farm fence, he saw a pig, a duck, and a cow reading in the sun.

The wolf had never seen animals read before. "I'm so hungry that my eyes are playing tricks on me," he said to himself. But he really was very hungry and didn't stop to think about it for long.

The wolf stood up tall, took a deep breath . . .

. . . and leaped at the animals with a howl—

"AaaOOOOOooo!"

Chickens and rabbits ran for their
lives, but the duck, the pig, and the cow didn't budge.
"What is that awful noise?" complained the cow.
"I can't concentrate on my book."
"Just ignore it," said the duck.

The wolf did not like to be ignored.

"What's wrong with you?" growled the wolf. "Can't you see I'm a big and dangerous wolf?"

"I'm sure you are," replied the pig. "But couldn't you be big and dangerous somewhere else? We're trying to read. This is a farm for educated animals. Now be a good wolf and go away," said the pig, giving him a push.

The wolf had never been treated like this before.

"Educated animals . . . educated animals!" the wolf repeated to himself. "This is something new. Well then! I'll learn how to read too." And off he went to school.

The children found it strange to have a wolf in their class, but since he didn't try to eat anyone, they soon got used to him. The wolf was serious and hardworking, and after much effort he learned to read and write. Soon he became the best in the class.

Feeling quite satisfied, the wolf went back to the farm and jumped over the fence. I'll show them, he thought.

He opened his book and began to read:

"Run, wolf! Run!
See wolf run."

"You've got a long way to go," said the duck, without even bothering to look up. And the pig, the duck, and the cow went on reading their own books, not the least impressed.

The wolf jumped back over the fence and ran straight to the public library. He studied long and hard, reading lots of dusty old books, and he practiced and practiced until he could read without stopping.

"They'll be impressed with my reading now," he said to himself.

The wolf walked up to the farm gate and knocked.
He opened *The Three Little Pigs* and began to read:

*"Onceuponatimetherewerethreelittlepigsonedaytheir
mothercalledthemandtoldthem—"*

"Stop that racket," interrupted the duck.
"You have improved," remarked the pig, "but you still
need to work on your style."
The wolf tucked his tail between his legs and slunk away.

But the wolf wasn't about to give up. He counted the little money he had left, went to the bookshop, and bought a splendid new storybook. His first very own book!

He was going to read it day and night, every letter and every line. He would read so well that the farm animals would admire him.

Ding-dong, rang the wolf at the farm gate.

He lay down on the grass, made himself comfortable, took out his new book, and began to read.

He read with confidence and passion, and the pig, the cow, and the duck all listened and said not one word.

Each time he finished a story, the pig, the duck, and the cow asked if he would please read them another.

So the wolf read on, story after story.
One minute he was Little Red Riding Hood,

the next a genie emerging
from a lamp,

and then a swashbuckling pirate.

"This is so much fun!" said the duck.

"He's a master," said the pig.

"Why don't you join us on our picnic
today?" offered the cow.

And so they all had a picnic—the pig, the duck, the cow, and the wolf. They lay in the tall grass and told stories all the afternoon long.

"We should all become storytellers," said the cow suddenly.

"We could travel around the world," added the duck.

"We can start tomorrow morning," said the pig.

The wolf stretched in the grass. He was happy to have such wonderful friends.